Class Picture Day

written by Margaret McNamara
illustrated by Mike Gordon

Ready-to-Read

Simon Spotlight
New York   London   Toronto   Sydney

For Emma

Simon Spotlight
An imprint of Simon & Schuster Children's Publishing Division
1230 Avenue of the Americas, New York, NY 10020
Text copyright © 2011 by Margaret McNamara
Illustrations copyright © 2011 by Mike Gordon
For information about special discounts for bulk purchases, please contact
Simon & Schuster Special Sales at 1-866-506-1949 or business@simonandschuster.com.
The Simon & Schuster Speakers Bureau can bring authors to your live event. For more
information or to book an event contact the Simon & Schuster Speakers Bureau at
1-866-248-3049 or visit our website at www.simonspeakers.com.
Manufactured in the United States 0511 LAK
2 4 6 8 10 9 7 5 3 1
Library of Congress Cataloging-in-Publication Data
McNamara, Margaret.
Smile! It's picture day / by Margaret McNamara ; illustrated by Mike Gordon.
p. cm. – (Robin Hill School) (Ready-to-read)
Summary: When Emma learns that her class picture will be taken while she must wear an
eye patch, she is sad because she will look different from the other first-graders.
ISBN 978-1-4169-9173-1 (pbk)
ISBN 978-1-4424-3611-4 (hc)
ISBN 978-1-4424-3517-9 (eBook)
[1. individuality–Fiction. 2. Schools–Fiction. 3. Photographs–Fiction.]
I. Gordon, Mike, 1948 Mar. 16- ill. II. Title.
PZ7.M47879343Smi 2011   [E]--dc22   2010030356

Emma was at the eye doctor.

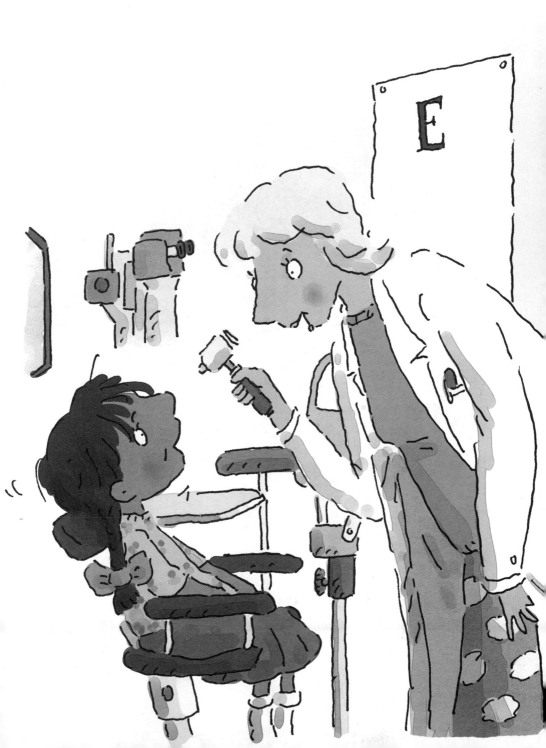

"Emma," said the doctor.

"We need to make

your right eye stronger."

The doctor put a patch
over Emma's left eye.

"Now your right eye
will do all the work,"
she said.

All the first graders
wanted to see
Emma's eye patch.

"You look like a pirate!"
said Eigen.

"Can I get one?"

asked Hannah.

Then Mrs. Connor said,
"Tomorrow is picture day."

"Tonight your homework
is to smile a lot."

Emma did not smile
when she got home.

"Tomorrow is picture day,"
she told her dad.
"And I have an eye patch!"

"I will look different
from all the other kids!"

Emma's dad gave her a hug.

"Different is not bad,"

he said.

"But it is different!"
said Emma.

That night,

Emma's dad stayed up late.

He worked on

a secret project.

The next day, Emma's dad
gave Mrs. Connor
his secret project.

Soon it was time

for the class picture.

Everybody lined up
in three rows.
James held a sign.

ROBIN HILL SCHOOL
GRADE 1
MRS. CONNOR
SPRING CLASS PICTURE

"Smile!"
said the photographer.
Everybody smiled,
except Emma.

"You are all done,"

said the photographer.

"Wait!" said Mrs. Connor.

"I have a surprise."

Mrs. Connor opened
the secret project box.
It was full of eye patches!

Mrs. Connor gave one
to each first grader . . .
except Emma.

Everyone put on

the eye patches.

"Smile again!"
said the photographer.

Everybody smiled
their biggest smiles.

And Emma's was
the biggest of all.